Little, Brown and Company

Hachette Book Group
1290 Avenue of the Americas, New York, NY 10104
Visit us at lb-kids.com
mylittlepony.com

Little, Brown and Company is a division of Hachette Book Group, Inc.
The Little, Brown name and logo are trademarks of Hachette Book Group, Inc.

The publisher is not responsible for websites (or their content) that are not owned by the publisher.

First Edition: April 2016

ISBN 978-0-316-38962-4

10 9 8 7 6 5 4 3 2 1

PHX

Printed in the United States of America

This book was edited by Mary-Kate Gaudet and designed by Christina Quintero.
The production was supervised by Rebecca Westall, and the production editor was Wendy Dopkin.

The illustrations for this book were created digitally. The text was set in Bembo, Love Potion Bold, and Girder Poster, and the display type is Mishka Regular. The pages were printed on text stock Influence Soft Gloss and ink as Flint Ink.

Licensed By:

Good Night, Baby Flurry Heart

By Michael Vogel
Illustrated by Amy Mebberson

Little, Brown and Company
New York Boston

Once upon a time, in the magical land of Equestria...

Two princesses stood high in a tower. Princess Celestia used her magic to lower the sun, while her sister, Princess Luna, used her magic to raise the moon. This let ponies across the land know it was time to sleep.

In the Crystal Empire, the Crystal Ponies saw the night sky and thanked Luna. Everypony was ready to get some good rest!

Well, *almost* everypony.

The royal baby, Princess Flurry Heart, was wide-awake. In fact, Princess Cadance and Shining Armor's daughter was not interested in going to sleep. *At. All.*

Shining Armor was at his wit's end. Telling soldiers what to do was *way* easier than telling his daughter to go to sleep!

He tried her favorite stuffed animal.

He tried singing a lullaby.

He even tried silly tricks!

But nothing worked! Flurry Heart just would not go to sleep!

Shining Armor had one last idea! He
would tell Flurry Heart a bedtime story.

*One that's exciting and daring and filled with
adventure!* he thought.

He tucked Flurry Heart
into her crib and started
his story the way *all* good
bedtime stories start:

Once upon a time...

...there lived a brave and daring young Unicorn who traveled all across Equestria in search of adventure. Though he battled timberwolves and cragadiles, he craved even *more* excitement!

One day, the Unicorn was traveling through the mysterious Everfree Forest when he came across a giant beanstalk that grew high into the sky.

"Aha!" said the Unicorn. "I bet there's a *truly epic* adventure at the top of this beanstalk! I'm going to climb it!"

And so he did!

When he reached the top, he found a castle far too big for a regular-size pony! The Unicorn watched as a giant pony peered out a window at Equestria far, far below.

"Soon I will climb down my beanstalk and steal the land from all the little ponies. I will take their gems and force them to make me dinner!" said the giant pony.

The Unicorn needed to save Equestria! But before he could attack, the giant sniffed the air and bellowed—

"Um, sweetie, what are you doing?"

Shining Armor turned to see Princess Cadance in Flurry Heart's nursery.
"I'm telling our daughter an exciting bedtime story filled with adventure
to get her to fall asleep!" he announced proudly.

Cadance looked down at their baby, who was staring wide-eyed at her father. "I love you, sweetheart, but you don't know the first thing about a good bedtime story for a baby princess."

"You think you can do better?" Shining Armor asked.

"I was Princess Twilight's foal-sitter. I told your sister more bedtime stories than I can count! Step aside and let a pro show you how it's done."

"Flurry Heart's bedtime story should be sweet and delightful and musical!"

She tucked Flurry Heart into her crib and started her story the way *all* good bedtime stories start:

Once upon a time...

...there was a young Alicorn princess who lived near the magical Everfree Forest. Everypony loved her because she had a beautiful singing voice and brought joy wherever she went. One day, she wandered deep into the forest and lost her way!

But before she could get *too* scared, seven cute little dragons came out of the shadows and asked if she was okay!

The princess explained that she needed to find her way back to her castle. The dragons were happy to help, but they asked if the princess would sing for them first.

♪!

And so she did.

The dragons were *so* happy that she had taken the time to sing for them, they gave her all the gems they were planning to eat for dinner.

She said she couldn't *possibly* take them, but the dragons—

"A pro, huh? You might want to take a look at your daughter, foal-sitter extraordinaire."

Cadance stopped her story and turned to see what Shining Armor was talking about.

Baby Flurry Heart wasn't in her crib! She had teleported across the bedroom and was sitting in the corner playing with her toys.

"You may have been good at telling Twily bedtime stories," Shining Armor said, "but our daughter felt your story was a little…dull."

"Your story had timberwolves and cragadiles!" Cadance retorted. "It would have kept her up *all* night! That's no way to get her to go to sleep!"

Shining Armor sighed. "Well, if my exciting story doesn't work and your sweet story doesn't work, how are we going to persuade Flurry Heart to go to sleep?"

Cadance had an idea. "What if we try both?"

"You mean a delightful adventure?" Shining Armor asked.

"Something exciting and musical!" replied Cadance.

They grinned at each other. "Daring *and* sweet!" they said at the same time.

And so Cadance and Shining Armor *both* tucked Flurry Heart in. And *this* time, they *both* began the story the way *all* good bedtime stories start:

Once upon a time...

...a dashing and daring Unicorn was traveling through the mystical and mysterious Everfree Forest in search of adventure when he was stopped by seven little dragons. Their friend, a beautiful Alicorn princess, had been ponynapped by a giant pony! He had heard her singing, locked her in a cage in his castle, and forced her to sing only for him!

The Unicorn agreed to help the dragons.
They took him through the forest to a clearing
where a giant beanstalk grew high into the
sky! They told him he would have to climb it
to find the princess.

And so he did.

The Unicorn climbed until he reached the giant pony's castle. He sneaked inside and found the princess. She was singing a sad, sad song. He told her not to worry; he was there to rescue her! The princess was thrilled and told him that the giant kept the key to her cage on a chain around his neck.

That night, the Unicorn waited for the giant to fall asleep. Then he very carefully slipped the key off the giant's neck and used it to free the princess!

They were about to escape when the giant woke up!

"FEE-FI-FONEY-BALONEY! YOU TOOK MY KEY, YOU LITTLE PONY!!!"

"Don't worry," said the princess. "I have an idea. We just need to—"

"Shhhhh! Honey, look!"

Shining Armor and Cadance looked into the crib. Princess Flurry Heart was fast asleep!

Cadance *slowly* covered Flurry Heart with a blanket. Shining Armor *carefully* arranged her favorite toys around her. They both *quietly* backed out of the bedroom, and Shining Armor *gently* shut the door.

Shining Armor turned to see Cadance looking at him.

"Well?" she asked.

"Well, what? We got Flurry Heart to go to sleep!"

"But we didn't finish the story!" Cadance said, smiling. "What happened to the Unicorn and the princess?"

Shining Armor grinned. "Well, I think the princess was about to reveal her brilliant plan to save them both from the giant."

"Yes," agreed Cadance. "And I think the Unicorn was going to do something *very* brave to get them safely back down the beanstalk."

"Definitely. And I'm pretty sure they fell in love."

"Then what?" asked Princess Cadance. "How does the story end?"

"The same way *every* good story ends, of course!"